S0-BKJ-305

The Howling Monkeys

Ray Carpenter's Expedition

by NANCY K. ROBINSON

Illustrated by BILL TINKER

SCHOLASTIC BOOK SERVICES

NEW YORK · TORONTO · LONDON · AUCKLAND · SYDNEY · TOKYO

This book is sold subject to the condition that it shall not be resold, lent, or otherwise circulated in any binding or cover other than that in which it is published — unless prior written permission has been obtained from the publisher — and without a similar condition, including this condition, being imposed on the subsequent purchaser.

Copyright © 1973 by Nancy K. Robinson. Illustrations© 1973 by Scholastic Magazines, Inc. All rights reserved. Published by Scholastic Book Services, a division of Scholastic Magazines, Inc.

1st printing ....January 1973

Printed in the U.S.A.

With deepest thanks to Dr. C. R. Carpenter (whose other name is Ray) and his wife, Ruth Carpenter.

RAY CARPENTER is a monkey observer.

What is an observer?

An observer is someone who watches. He knows how to watch things or animals or even other people. A good observer watches and looks and listens for a very long time before he believes his eyes and ears. A good observer knows it is easy to make mistakes.

Sometimes it is hard to be an observer. Once a scientist tried to observe a monkey in a laboratory. He wanted to find out how the monkey behaved when it was alone — when it did not know it was being watched.

So he put the monkey behind a screen. Then he made a tiny peephole in the screen. "Now the monkey won't be able to see me," he thought.

But every time the scientist looked through the peephole, there was the monkey, peeping out at him.

Then the scientist got a better idea. He closed up the peephole and put a mirror above his workbench. When he looked in the mirror, he could see what was going on behind him, on the other side of the screen. "Now," he thought, "I'll find out how a monkey really behaves."

But almost at once the monkey spied the mirror. From that moment on, whenever the scientist looked in the mirror at the monkey, he saw the monkey looking in the mirror at him. That's all the monkey ever did. He watched the scientist in the mirror while the scientist watched him.

This is the story of another scientist who observed monkeys in a laboratory. But he did more than that. He set out alone to observe monkeys in their jungle homes. He was one of the first people to do this.

Ray Carpenter

RAY CARPENTER wanted to know everything about monkeys. He had hundreds of questions. How do monkeys find food? How do they eat and sleep? What do they do all day long? How do they take care of their babies? How do they get along with each other? Do they fight a lot?

He wanted to know how monkeys lived —

not in the zoo,

not in the circus,

not even in a scientific laboratory.

He wanted to know how monkeys lived at home in the jungle.

But first Ray watched monkeys in the scientific laboratory at Yale University, where he worked as a scientist. He also read dozens of books about monkeys, but none of them ever answered all of his questions. Professor Robert M. Yerkes, who was in charge of the laboratory, couldn't answer all of his questions either.

Two scientists had tried to study chimpanzees and gorillas in Africa, but they had come back without learning much. The year was 1931 and monkey behavior was still a big mystery.

Professor Yerkes heard that a place called Barro Colorado Island might be a good place to learn about a special kind of monkey called a howling monkey. He heard about this from another scientist named Dr. Frank N. Chapman who studied birds on the island.

Who could go to the island to observe the howling monkeys?

One day Professor Yerkes came into the laboratory with a letter in his hand. The letter was from a man who had been Ray's teacher.

The letter said, "If anyone can learn about monkeys, Ray Carpenter can. Ray is one of the hardest workers I have ever seen. He is an excellent observer."

Professor Yerkes showed Ray the letter. "How would you like to go to Barro Colorado Island?" he asked Ray. "How would you like to live on this island for a year and spend every day with monkeys?"

Ray was so excited, he couldn't say a word.

Barro Colorado Island

BEFORE Ray knew it, he was on the biggest adventure of his life. On a freezing cold December day he left New York City on a United Fruit Company boat.

After five days and five nights, the boat arrived in Panama and Ray changed to a smaller lake boat. Soon the lake boat docked at Barro Colorado Island, a beautiful island covered with thick tropical rain forest. The water was bright blue and the sun was hot.

When Ray stepped off the lake boat, he climbed up 196 steps. At the top, a pleasant-looking man with a white moustache met him and shook his hand. This was Dr. Chapman, the man who told Professor Yerkes about the howling monkeys.

"Well," said Dr. Chapman with a twinkle in his eye, "the howlers are waiting to greet you."

Ray forgot about his trunk and his baggage and gear. He forgot how tired he was after the long trip. Quickly he followed Dr. Chapman. They walked behind a small group of houses and into the rain forest.

Suddenly Dr. Chapman stopped and pointed up. Ray looked up. High in the trees overhead, he saw dark shapes moving slowly along the branches. Just then one of the dark shapes dropped and hung by its tail from a branch. Slowly

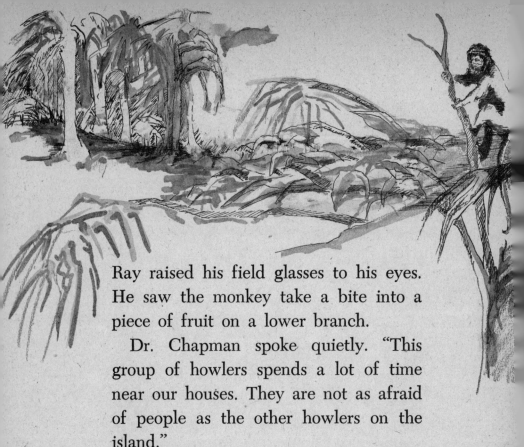

Ray raised his field glasses to his eyes. He saw the monkey take a bite into a piece of fruit on a lower branch.

Dr. Chapman spoke quietly. "This group of howlers spends a lot of time near our houses. They are not as afraid of people as the other howlers on the island."

For a long time Dr. Chapman watched Ray watching the monkeys. Then he went into one of the houses.

Hours went by. Ray never moved from the spot. He had never seen so many monkeys at one time. He wondered if this was a family. No — there were too many monkeys. He decided to try to count them.

Just then he heard a sound behind him in the forest. The forest was beautiful, but it was a little scary too. Suddenly he remembered that there were many wild animals on Barro Colorado Island — pumas, tapirs, ocelots, and poisonous snakes. What was that strange noise?

Then he heard a voice. "Merry Christmas!" Ray turned around. He saw a man carrying a big tray. It was Nico, the cook.

"Merry Christmas?"

Ray looked at the tray. It was filled with pieces of turkey breast and stuffing, sweet potatoes and pudding. Then Ray looked at the high green trees, the colorful birds and the bright blue sky through the trees. It didn't look like Christmas. But it was December 25, 1931. Ray took a deep breath and smelled the flowers he had never smelled before and the strange animal smells. He was in the tropics.

The Monkeys

EARLY the next morning Ray found out how howling monkeys got their name. He woke up at 5:15 and listened. The forest was full of sounds. The night animals were going to sleep and the day animals were waking up. Then from far away he heard a low grunt. Uh uh uh. It grew louder and faster. Slowly it rose to a long ferocious roar, as loud as a lion or an elephant. The roaring and howling went on for many minutes. Then, all at once, it stopped.

Ray sat up in his cot and looked around. There were six other scientists fast asleep on the sleeping porch. They had come to Barro Colorado Island to study the flowers, plants, insects and the other animals. Ray looked out at the lake. He saw the lights of a ship on its way through the Panama Canal.

Then the grunts began again. This time they came from another place. Another group of howlers was waking up. Quickly Ray put on his shorts and his shirt and his heavy shoes. He packed everything he thought he needed for a day in the tropical forest.

Field glasses to see the monkeys

Pocket notebook and pencil to make notes about what he saw

Camera to take pictures of the monkeys

Machete (large knife) to cut through the bushes

Pistol in case he met a dangerous animal or needed to signal for help

Snake kit and antitoxin in case he got bitten

Clean cloths to use as bandages

Canteen with water

Map of the island with trails marked to know where he was going so he wouldn't get lost

Compass in case he did get lost

Waterproof bag to keep the other things dry in case it rained (It probably wouldn't rain. Ray had come to the island at the beginning of the dry season.)

Ray hoped he was ready for anything. He went to the tree where he had seen howlers the day before. There he stopped and waited. Everything was quiet. He wondered if the monkeys had gone away. Then he heard low clucking sounds. He was very near the howlers! In a tree nearby he saw them. He was almost sure they were the same group he watched the day before. When they began howling, he moved closer and hid behind a tree. Slowly he raised his field glasses to his eyes and focused them on the monkeys high up in the branches.

Ray looked up through the leaves and the branches. He didn't know where to start.

"I'll just count them," he said to himself. "Now there's one female sitting on a branch with a small howler playing near her legs." He wrote in his notebook:

one female

one infant

When he looked up again, there were four monkeys chasing each other around. Or were there five? He saw another female. "No," he thought, "I've already counted her." A monkey moved slowly out on a branch, but Ray couldn't tell if it was a male or a female.

He was getting all mixed up. All the younger monkeys looked alike. "What kind of scientist am I if I can't even count monkeys?" he asked himself.

Then he saw a female howler resting on her back in the fork of a branch. Her legs and stomach formed a sort of basket. And there was something in the basket. Two tiny eyes were blinking out at Ray. It was a baby howler waking up.

A large male howler walked out on the same branch. Ray watched him move. He was big and slow. His tail was as long as he was and it was always wrapped around a limb. The hair around his neck was long and reddish, but the rest of him was black. He had a bushy beard. He passed the mother and the baby and kept moving out on the branch.

He stopped and bit into a wild fig. Then he moved to another branch and nibbled again. He was getting farther and farther away from the group and closer and closer to Ray. Ray looked hard through his field glasses. It didn't seem as if the howler was really eating. Was he just pretending to eat so he could get a better look at Ray? Now Ray could see the howler's face quite well. And he looked fiercely handsome.

Ray tried not to move at all. He didn't want to frighten the howler and he didn't want the howler to think he was an enemy.

He held very still.

Then the howler did a funny thing. He yawned. But he didn't seem sleepy. He didn't seem bored. He seemed very excited. The other monkeys stopped what they were doing and watched. Then the howler yawned again — right at Ray.

Ray didn't know what to do. The field glasses began to feel very heavy — so heavy that his arms were shaking. Ray didn't think he could hold still for another second. But he did.

He held still for an hour.

At the end of the hour the monkey turned his back on Ray. Now he couldn't see Ray at all and he didn't seem so excited.

Ray took a deep breath and dropped his arms. He had never done such hard work in his life.

But the next minute Ray lifted his field glasses again. Something was happening. The male monkeys were moving around as if they were looking for something. At the same time some of the males were making deep clucking noises. It was a different noise from the grunts and howls he had heard earlier that morning.

All at once two male monkeys started

off through the trees, one behind the other. They made some deep clucking noises again and looked back at the others. A mother monkey started to move. Her baby jumped quickly on her back and wrapped its little tail around her big tail. They followed the two leaders.

Another female came next, followed by a young howler. When the young howler came to a difficult crossing between two trees, he waited for his mother to make a bridge with her tail, body and arms. Then he scurried across her tail and her back.

The monkeys were moving in a single file through the trees. Ray suddenly laughed out loud. If they always moved like this — single file, one behind the other — he would be able to count them.

Attack

RAY COUNTED 25 monkeys that day. When he got back to the house, he was tired and very hungry. He remembered to bring a canteen of water into the forest, but he hadn't brought a thing to eat.

But what bothered him most was that he was itching all over. He had been ready for attacks by snakes and large dangerous animals, but he hadn't been ready for the attack of a very small animal. That animal was the tick. Ticks belong to the spider family, but they are much smaller than spiders. They attach themselves to people and animals by biting into the skin and sucking the blood. They can be very painful.

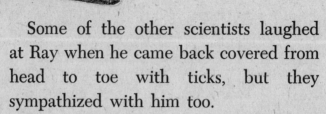

Some of the other scientists laughed at Ray when he came back covered from head to toe with ticks, but they sympathized with him too.

When Ray tried to pull the ticks off, the heads stayed under his skin. He finally had to cut them out with a knife.

"Ray, you can't wear clothes like that," said Dr. Chapman. Ray looked down at the light shirt and shorts he had put on that day, thinking he would be cool. Dr. Chapman wore heavy khaki clothes with his pants tucked into his shoes.

Ray didn't get much sleep that night. He was itching all over.

The next day Ray took a boat to Panama. He found a store that sold heavy khaki clothing. He bought a heavy shirt with long sleeves. He bought trousers and hiking shoes and thick socks.

When he got back to the island, he put on his new outfit. He tucked the trousers into the socks. Then he put adhesive tape around the top of the socks. His whole body was covered. He was ready to go into the forest again. "This time," Ray thought, "the ticks won't bother me."

But he was wrong. By the end of the second day he learned that ticks can get through openings in clothing. Somehow or other, they climbed in around his belt, his shoe tops, and his neck. Worst of all, they stayed in his clothes overnight and he couldn't get them out.

When he talked to the other scientists, he found out that they had the same problem, but since they didn't spend so much time in the forest, the ticks didn't bother them so much.

But they bothered Ray. He didn't get much sleep. The itching got worse and worse. Ray knew that a good observer must be comfortable to observe.

He had to do something about the ticks.

Ray had learned that ticks are *negatively geotropic*. This means that they climb upwards away from the ground whenever they can.

One night he was looking at his clothes hanging over the back of a chair. He thought, "Maybe I can get the ticks out of my clothing if I give them someplace to climb up."

Ray found a piece of wire and made a loop at the end. He put his shirt and pants on a wire hanger. Then he hung the hanger on the loop.

The next morning the wire hanger was covered with ticks of many sizes. They had found a place to climb! His idea had worked.

When the other scientists saw how Ray got the ticks out of his clothing, they did the same thing to get rid of their ticks.

A Decision

RAY HAD to make a decision. What to do first. He wondered if he should go out right away and try to find all the howlers that lived on Barro Colorado Island.

He thought hard and long about this. He didn't know the island very well. Even though the island was small, trails went all over the place. He might spend hours and hours just looking for monkeys.

Then he thought about the group who lived near the houses — the group he had already seen and counted. This group he called Group I.

"What if I follow Group I every day for at least one whole month?" he asked himself. "What if I study what they do from minute to minute and from hour to hour? Maybe I would get to know them and find out what they do all day."

So every day from dawn to dusk for a month Ray followed Group I. In the beginning he wasn't always sure it was Group I. So one of the first things he did was to count the monkeys because he knew there were about 25 monkeys in Group I. Soon he began to recognize some of the monkeys. Whenever he saw those monkeys he knew he was looking at Group I.

Every day he spent ten or more hours with Group I. As the month went by, he slowly realized that his plan was working. He was finding out what Group I did all day long.

Howler Schedule

SUNRISE. Between five and six o'clock in the morning the monkeys wake up and howl. Ray wakes up too and quickly gets dressed. Then he waits.

Far away he hears the roars of one group. A few minutes later another group starts howling. When Ray hears the howls very close by, he knows Group I is waking up. He follows the sound and the smell of the monkeys and tries to reach them before they have finished their morning howls. The reason he does this is that he finds he can get closer to the howlers while they are howling. The noise they are making covers up the noise Ray is making. Also, because they are so busy howling, they seem to pay less attention to Ray.

Usually he finds them in the same tree he left them in the night before. Ray calls this tree where the howlers sleep the *lodge tree*. For several nights Group I chooses the same lodge tree.

When the monkeys finish their morning howls, they eat a little and then rest in the same tree. They might nibble a leaf or two, but mostly they rest. In the middle of the morning some of the adult males begin to make deep, hoarse clucking sounds. It is time for the march.

Ray tries to find a good position to count the monkeys. But he wants to do more than just count them. He wants to find out what monkey goes first. How many times does that monkey go first? What monkey goes second? How many times does that monkey go second? Which monkey goes third and so on all the way up to which monkey goes 25th and how many times is that monkey in the last place in line.

The morning march ends up at a feeding tree. The feeding tree is often a wild fig tree. Wild figs seem to be their favorite food. The howlers usually feed until about 11 o'clock in the morning. But if there is a lot of fruit around they might get enough to eat sooner and so finish earlier.

The howlers hardly ever pick the food with their hands. Often they hang upside down by their tails and bite right into a piece of fruit growing on a branch below. Sometimes they pull a branch over with their feet and then put their mouths to the food they want to eat on that branch.

Ray observes that mother howlers do pick fruit and leaves. They might eat a little of it themselves and then, as they are holding the food in their hands, their babies taste it. This is the way baby howlers learn that there are good things to eat besides the milk they suck from their mothers' nipples.

Ray keeps a list of everything the howlers eat. Here are the ways he finds out what they eat:

He watches them eat. If he doesn't know the name of the leaf or fruit they are eating, he carefully picks some and puts a label on it. On the label he writes a number. Then he places it in his waterproof bag. Later he will send it to a scientist in Chicago who is an expert on plants and leaves of Central America. The scientist will write back what the plant or fruit is. Then Ray will put its name on his list.

Often he cannot see what they are eating. He has other ways of finding out what food howlers like. One way is to study the pieces of food the howlers have wasted. And howlers are very wasteful. Sometimes they take only a bite or two from a large leaf or piece of fruit and let the rest drop to the ground.

The third way to find out what howlers eat is to examine the howler's fecal matter. In the fecal matter there will be traces of the food the howlers have eaten the day before.

Howlers eat juicy leaves, berries, flowers, buds, fruits, and parts of nuts. After the morning feeding period there is a rest period during the middle of the day.

But not all the howlers rest. The little ones don't seem to rest very much all day. They wrestle with each other and chase each other around on the branches. The older howlers don't seem to mind unless the games get too rough. Then an adult male might growl and the young monkeys calm down a little.

In the middle of the afternoon there is often another march to another food tree. After they have eaten some more and rested, there is another march. This time it is to the lodge tree where they will spend the night. They usually arrive at the lodge tree before six and settle themselves on the branches. Before seven o'clock at night most of the howlers are resting or sleeping.

And so the howlers' day comes to an end. At night they wake up and move a little. If it rains, the males may wake up and roar for a little while.

Questions, Answers, and Guesses

RAY WAS beginning to find answers to some of the questions on his long list of questions. He was beginning to answer two of the biggest: "What do howlers do all day long?" and the other, "How do they adapt themselves to their jungle home?"

But a funny thing was happening. The more answers he found, the more questions he needed to ask.

Whenever he observed something that the monkeys did again and again, he could almost be sure he had an answer to his question. But for many of the questions he had no sure answers. And for a few questions he made guesses about the answers until he could be sure.

*Did the same monkey lead
the march every day?*

No. But fifteen times an adult male
went first. An adult female without a
baby went first five times and a female
carrying a baby went first four times. Ray
could say that an adult male went first
more than any other monkey, but it wasn't
always the same adult male.

Do howler monkeys fight over food?

Ray didn't see any howlers fight over
food. So far he had seen no fighting at
all between howlers, although the young
howlers did a lot of rough play-fighting.

Why do howlers waste so much food?

Ray made guesses about the answer to
this question. One reason they might
waste so much food is that there seemed

to be plenty of food around and they didn't have to worry about running out. This might also explain why they didn't have to fight over food. There was always enough for everyone.

But another kind of answer Ray thought of was that howlers just were not very careful eaters. They didn't use their hands much when they ate. Ray had seen other kinds of monkeys in the laboratory at Yale who did use their hands when they ate. Those monkeys often held a piece of fruit in their hands and picked it with their fingers. Ray hardly ever saw howlers do that. This led to an important question —

Why don't howlers use their hands to eat?

Ray noticed something funny about the howler's hand. The howler has a thumb and four fingers just like us. But the howler's thumb is very small and does not

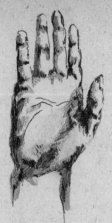

work the way our thumb works.

People and many kinds of monkeys and apes have what scientists call *opposable thumbs*. Opposable thumbs are very useful for picking up small things. But a howler's thumb sticks up just like the other fingers.

So Ray made a guess. He guessed that a howler's hands are not very useful for picking and holding food. It's just too hard! This might also explain why howlers do not spend much time picking dirt and insects out of their fur as many other monkeys do.

A howler's hand may not be very good for holding food, but it is just right for traveling over branches.

How do howlers get water to drink?

Ray was puzzled about this. He knew all monkeys needed water, but he never saw howlers coming to the ground and drinking from a stream. Why weren't the monkeys very thirsty? Ray couldn't figure it out. Then one day he realized that much of the food the monkeys ate — fruit, buds, and leaves — were made mostly of water and they didn't really need more than that.

A few months later, during the rainy season, he found that howlers also drink rainwater. They lick the rain water right off the leaves of the trees or they wipe it up along the branches and carry it to their mouths.

Do howlers ever walk on the ground?

Ray did not see any howlers walking on the ground. Mostly they walked on all four feet along the top of a branch, except when they wanted to swing from one tree to another.

How do howlers use their tails?

Ray saw tails used in many ways. Usually they were wrapped around a branch to catch the monkey in case it slipped and fell. A small monkey used its tail to hold on to its mother when riding on her back.

Sometimes the tails were used to explore in the same way an elephant uses his trunk. On the tip of the tail there was no hair. This part of the tail could feel things better than the hairy part.

A mother howler might use her tail to help form a bridge at a crossing between two trees. Then a young howler who was afraid to jump could run across her back.

Tails were also good for flicking away insects and flies.

A newborn baby's tail might be very useful to its mother. Once Ray saw a mother howler holding a tiny grayish infant by its tail and licking it clean. It was the baby's first bath!

*How do howlers sleep? Do
they ever build nests?*

When it was time for bed or a rest,
howlers usually lay along a branch on
their stomachs, backs, or sides and
wrapped their tails around another
branch. Tiny babies slept in a sort of
basket formed by their mothers' laps.
When the babies got a little older, they
slept with their arms and legs all wrapped
up with their mothers' arms and legs.

Ray never saw howlers build nests.
They didn't change anything on the tree
to make a bed. They didn't even bend
down a twig that was sticking up. But
they did pick comfortable places in the
tree to sleep — places where two branches
came together and there were lots of
twigs. Well, comfortable, that is, for
howlers.

Howling

Ray wanted to know what the howlers were saying when they howled. The first question he asked himself was, "Why do howlers howl at the beginning of day? Are they just howling at the sun coming up?"

No, that wasn't a very good answer because each group howled at a slightly different time. Ray began to think that each group was telling something to the other groups of howlers. He thought they were saying, "We're here!"

But it seemed they must be saying more than that.

Maybe they were saying, "We're here! We're going to fight you."

Maybe they were saying, "We're here! Don't come any closer."

After a while Ray guessed that each group was telling the other groups their plans for the rest of the morning. For even though a group of howlers might take a different route from the day before, they hardly ever came near the other groups of howlers and the other groups hardly ever came near them.

One morning Ray woke up late. Right away he could tell something was wrong. The howlers were still howling and it was the loudest howling he had ever heard. He rushed out to find Group I. When he got there, he saw another group of howlers very close by.

All the monkeys were very excited. The male howlers in both groups were dashing back and forth, roaring with all their might. The females were all barking and the young howlers were whining.

The excitement lasted for two whole hours. Then the strange group of howlers moved away. Group I calmed down and went on with their daily activities. Ray thought to himself, "I have seen a battle!"

Ray thought that Group I had won the battle because the strange group had moved away. He looked at the map he had made of Group I's movements over the last few weeks.

Every time he found Group I, Ray had put a little dot on his map to show where he had found them that day, where they had fed and where they had slept. Then Ray drew a line connecting all the dots. This area he called "home range."

Ray had seen Group I take marches outside of this area, but when they went far from home range, they seemed less sure of themselves. They moved more slowly through the trees. And they seemed to have trouble deciding which monkey was leading the march. Inside the area called "home range" the monkeys in Group I moved faster through the trees. They seemed to know what they were doing.

Ray looked at this map and thought about what had happened that morning. He guessed that the strange group of howlers had come too near Group I's home range. And that was why there had been a battle.

But it was a strange kind of battle. There had been no real fighting and no one got hurt. It was a battle of howls. Ray couldn't help thinking, "What a good way to settle an argument."

A few weeks later Ray heard howling again. This time it was in the middle of the morning. He rushed out thinking that the strange group had come too close again, but when he got there he found only one strange howler all alone in a tree near Group I. All the males in Group I were howling at him. The strange howler had a big cut on his leg and Ray wondered if he had been bitten.

For a few days this strange howler followed Group I around and they howled at him and dropped branches on him. Then one day the howling stopped. Ray thought the strange howler had gone back to the forest to live alone. But when he counted the howlers in Group I, there were 26!

The strange howler had finally joined the group.

The monkeys howled in the morning. They howled when another group of howlers came too close. They howled at the rain and at large birds and airplanes. And they sometimes howled at Ray.

There was another time too when the howls seemed to mean something special. This is what Ray thought they meant: *"Baby falling!"*

When baby howlers are born, they are able to hold on very tight. During the first month, they ride holding on to the long hairs on their mothers' stomachs where it is the warmest.

But soon they are riding on their mothers' backs with their tails wrapped around the base of their mothers' tails. And this is the time when most accidents happen.

One day Ray heard the sound of a breaking branch. Then he heard three weak shrieks that sounded like a call for help. A young howler had fallen to the ground.

Almost at the same time all the males in the group started a terrific roar and turned back. The mother of the fallen howler began to wail. She ended each wail with a grunt and a groan.

A male and a female howler began to climb carefully down a vine which hung close to the fallen howler. They waited.

Then, all at once, the female dashed down the vine to a bush, took the small howler on her back and returned to the tree tops and the rest of the group.

Ray observed that sometimes just the sound of a breaking branch could start all the males howling.

Tricks

Now it was time for Ray Carpenter to check his observations. Now it was time for him to find the other groups of howlers on the island to see if they behaved the same way as Group I.

At first Ray got lost. So for the next few weeks he studied all the trails on the island.

But the monkeys did not follow the trails on Ray's map. They had their own trails that went through the trees. Ray would have to learn these trails too. During this time Ray often felt discouraged. He was beginning all over again. The work was hard and he was always alone.

Ray did find the other groups of howlers. In the beginning it was sometimes hard to see them. When he came near, they ran away to the highest trees, hid, and kept very quiet. He would wait and they would wait for hours and hours.

Other groups howled at him. They broke branches off the trees and dropped them down at him. Another thing they did was to urinate and defecate on Ray.

At first Ray thought they did that because they were frightened. He knew that many animals urinated or defecated when they were scared.

But Ray noticed that their aim was very good. He was often hit on the head or shoulders with urine and fecal matter. Animals that are frightened usually try to get away in a hurry. But these howlers would stop, one after the other, and drop urine and fecal matter on Ray. Ray began to think that the howlers used their own urine and fecal matter as a kind of weapon, just as they dropped down branches and limbs.

Ray tried different tricks. He tried to trick the howlers into thinking he wasn't there.

One trick was to use green burlap and twigs to build a blind, a covering under which Ray hid himself. He hoped the howlers would think it was just another bush in the forest.

But most of the time the blinds did not fool the howlers. They would roar at the blinds, drop branches down on them and then, one after the other, drop fecal matter and urine on them.

Ray had another trick. He would hide half of his body behind a tree and then the monkeys wouldn't notice him as much as when all of him showed. This trick worked a little better.

But most of his tricks didn't work well at all. In fact, one day a group of howlers played a trick on Ray.

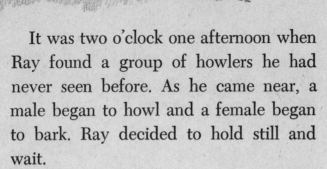

It was two o'clock one afternoon when Ray found a group of howlers he had never seen before. As he came near, a male began to howl and a female began to bark. Ray decided to hold still and wait.

After a while they calmed down. Then the male started to make clucking noises. They were about to march. Ray quickly found a hiding place under the line of march. He wanted to count them. It was a big group and they were moving through the trees. All at once the male and the female who were leading stopped. They turned around. Then the whole group turned around and began to march in the opposite direction — away from Ray.

Ray ran to find a new place under the monkeys. He took out his little notebook and pencil and began to count:

One male

one female

another male...

But then they stopped again and took off in a new direction. Ray tried to find another hiding place. By now he was huffing and puffing.

As soon as he had hidden himself the three leading monkeys stopped again. The whole group stopped. What were they doing?

Ray decided not to move any more. He waited and a few minutes later the two leading males and the female with a last barking growl started off again. This time they didn't stop. "This time it's for real," thought Ray.

Off the three monkeys went through the trees. But no monkeys followed them.

In fact there were no other monkeys in sight. Where were the rest of the monkeys? Everything was quiet.

Ray was getting suspicious. Had the other monkeys left while he was busy watching the leaders? Or were they hiding someplace hoping Ray would follow the leaders?

Ray waited. An hour went by. From far away he heard the clucking noises of the leading monkeys. Ray thought, "I have been fooled. The monkeys have all left." He started to get up. He was about to leave.

Just then he saw one of the leaders return quietly to the tree. One by one the rest of the group came out of the tree. They had been hiding quietly near Ray all this time! The three leading monkeys had made a large circle through the forest. Maybe they were hoping to lead Ray away from the rest of the group. They came back, as if they thought they had fooled him.

And they almost had.

As time went by the monkeys got used to Ray. They began to behave almost as if he weren't there. Ray gave up most of his tricks and acted more and more like himself. The monkeys gave up most of their tricks too and let Ray get closer and closer.

He was careful not to get too close. A good observer must not interfere too much with the animals he is observing.

Play

WHAT RAY liked best of all was watching the young howlers play. And they played most of the day. The littlest howlers never went far from their mothers. They played with their own feet and tails. They played with small branches or leaves nearby. They climbed all over their mothers.

But as they got older, they played with the other howlers. Here are some of the games Ray saw them play:

Two small monkeys are trying to force each other off a branch. One monkey pretends to fall, but catches himself just in time by his tail and hangs upside down. Then he climbs back on the branch and starts again.

Four young howlers are swinging upside down by their tails, wrestling and nipping each other while they hang.

Six howlers are chasing one another. They run along a branch, one behind the other, and then leap down to a lower branch. Then they follow the leader along the branch and swing up again. Round and round they go. Sometimes one howler grabs the tail of another one to keep him from running. Other times one monkey will lie in wait for another monkey. When the monkey comes past, he jumps on him.

Young howlers make chirping squeals as they play. If they are getting too rough and noisy a male adult nearby growls. Then they calm down a little.

Sometimes a lot of smaller monkeys would gang up on a bigger monkey. Even though Ray saw a lot of play-fighting, he hardly ever saw one monkey *really* try to

hurt another monkey. But one time it was
different.

A young howler was following a female
with an infant on her back. Ray wasn't
sure, but he thought this female was the
young howler's mother and the infant was
his new baby brother or sister.

The young howler started hitting the
infant and then tried to pull it off the
female's back. The infant bit the young
howler in the face and then slipped and

fell to a lower branch. Luckily it didn't fall very far and climbed up again quickly. The mother turned around. She raised herself and looked very hard at the young howler who had hit the baby. The young howler went away.

But a few minutes later, Ray saw the same young howler. He had found another female with a baby and he was hitting and pulling that baby.

Ray thought that young howlers learned a lot when they were playing and play-fighting. They learned who was stronger. They learned who was faster. But mostly they learned to know every monkey in their group. Most of the monkeys would live their whole lives in the same group. They would have to learn to get along with every other monkey in the group. So it is important to get to know one another.

Chita

RAY WANTED a pet howler. He wanted to see how a monkey behaves close up.

One night after supper, Dr. Chapman invited Ray to join him on his evening walk. Ray always enjoyed walking with Dr. Chapman. Dr. Chapman knew more about birds than anyone Ray had ever met. When they walked they looked for the big birds that came out in the evening and Dr. Chapman would imitate their sounds. But tonight they talked about Ray's wish for a pet howler.

Dr. Chapman listened and then he told Ray the story of a little howler named Claudia.

Claudia was a baby when Dr. Chapman found her. He kept her in a cage, but she never became tame. A tame animal can usually tell the difference between the person who feeds it and other people. But Claudia didn't seem to want to eat much and she didn't seem to pay any attention to Dr. Chapman.

Every day, when she heard the howls of her group, she howled back. Dr. Chapman was afraid to set her free. He was afraid her group would not take her back. He was afraid she would not know how to get along in the jungle and that she would die.

One day Dr. Chapman came to the cage and found Claudia dead. He never found out why she died. He wondered if she had died of a broken heart.

Ray thought about that story. He knew that howlers are never found in zoos. They hardly ever live long in captivity. He thought about what he had seen on Barro Colorado Island. Living in a group seemed to be very important to howlers. Ray decided to stop thinking about getting a howler for a pet.

But one day he came across a baby howler lying in some bushes on the ground. A big male monkey came halfway down a vine, then climbed up again. Ray went over to the baby howler. It was stunned and bleeding. He waited, but no monkey came down to get it. Finally he picked the baby up and carried it back to the house.

For the next few days Ray nursed the baby howler. She grew stronger and wanted to go everyplace with Ray. So Ray took her along draped around his neck like a scarf. He grew very fond of her and called her Chita.

Ray learned some new things about howlers from Chita. He could study her face close up and try to learn what she was saying with her face. He also learned from Chita that baby howlers purr. When they like what is being done to them, and feel calm and comfortable, they purr, just like kittens. When a baby howler purrs it can be a signal to the mother that the infant is happy.

Chita was a good friend and a good helper. When it came time for Ray Carpenter to leave the island, he took Chita back to Yale University along with a baby spider monkey named Chipper. The two monkeys lived in a cage in his office while he wrote a book about howlers.

When Ray Carpenter got back to the United States, he found that scientists were very excited about the work he had done on his trip. They were already planning to send Ray on more expeditions to study other kinds of monkeys and apes. Ray was excited too. He knew his observations of howlers would have to be checked again and again to see if they were true. But he knew his trip to Barro Colorado Island had proved something.

It had proved that it was possible to study monkeys in their jungle homes.